# CHOOSE YOUR O

MW00952656

## Kids Love Reading
### *Choose Your Own Adventure*®!

---

I LOVE *Choose Your Own Adventure* books
because I take risks but if something bad happens
I don't actually have something bad happen to
me. I feel like I'm actually there. I like being
able to choose what happens.
**Eli Askew, age 8**

---

You never know what's going to happen next!
**Skylar Stoudt, age 8**

---

Fun adventures and excitement!
**Tallulah Wible, age 8**

---

I love that I can choose if sometimes I want to take a
risk or sometimes want to be safe. *Choose Your Own
Adventures* are different than regular books.
**Fiona Wanner, age 8**

Illustrated by Manuel Mal
Book design by Stacey Boyd, Big Eyedea Visual Design
For information regarding permission, write to:

CHOOSECO

P.O. Box 46, Waitsfield, Vermont 05673
www.cyoa.com

A DRAGONLARK BOOK

Publisher's Cataloging-In-Publication Data
(Prepared by The Donohue Group, Inc.)

Names: Jones, Kyandreia, author. | Mal, Manuel, illustrator.
Title: The ghost on the mountain / by Kyandreia Jones ; illustrated by Manuel Mal.
Other Titles: Choose own adventure. Dragonlarks.
Description: Waitsfield, Vermont : Chooseco, [2022] | Series: Choose your own adventure | Series: A Dragonlark book | Interest age level: 005-008. | Summary: "The Ghost on the Mountain ... takes YOU on an adventure to Haiti, where you're spending the summer with your Grandma Yolette to learn about your heritage. You will discover the secrets that lie inside of your family and deep in the soil of the enchanting land"-- Provided by publisher.
Identifiers: ISBN 9781954232068 (paperback)
Subjects: LCSH: Grandparent and child--Haiti--Juvenile fiction. | Secrecy--Juvenile fiction. | Haiti--Description and travel--Juvenile fiction. | CYAC: Grandparent and child--Haiti--Fiction. | Family secrets--Fiction. | Haiti--Description and travel--Fiction. | LCGFT: Action and adventure fiction. | Choose-your-own stories.
Classification: LCC PZ7.1.J722 Gh 2022 | DDC [E]--dc23

Published simultaneously in the United States and Canada

Printed in China
10 9 8 7 6 5 4 3 2 1

# CHOOSE YOUR OWN ADVENTURE®

# The Ghost on the Mountain

## BY KYANDREIA JONES

### ILLUSTRATED BY MANUEL MAL

A DRAGONLARK BOOK

*in loving memory of*
*my grandma Yolette Milord*
*(1959–2009)*
*and*
*in honor of my Haitian ancestors*

WATCH OUT!
THIS BOOK IS DIFFERENT
from every book you've ever read.

Do not read this book from the first page
through to the last page.
Instead, start on page 1 and read until you
come to your first choice. Then turn to the
page shown and see what happens.

When you come to the end of a story,
you can go back and start again.
Every choice leads to a new adventure.

Good luck!

It is a hot August night in Haiti. Your mom sent you here to spend the summer with your Grandma Yolette and learn about where she is from. You took a small plane to the mountainous island.

And now you are in a small bedroom where it is very hot. And you know what else? You think this small bedroom has a ghost in it!

*Turn to the next page.*

You sit up to get a better look. There is a glowing woman in the middle of your room. You don't make a peep. Are ghosts normal here?

You wish you had asked your mom more questions before you left.

The ghost does not look like a ghost from a movie. She has long white dreadlocks, gray eyes, and brilliant skin. She seems friendly. She looks at you with a wide smile and bright, round eyes.

*Non mwen se Yvette. My name is Yvette.*

Her lips do not move, but you can hear her voice clearly. She has a thick accent like your grandmother's. The sound of her voice startles you. You grab your pet iguana, Crikey, and run out of the room.

*Turn to page 4.*

OOF! You run directly into your grandma's arms. Grandma Yolette lights a candle. Now you can see her soft, kind face in the dark hallway.

"What's the matter?" asks Grandma Yolette.

"There's a ghost!" you shout. "My room is haunted!"

"Haunted?"

Grandma Yolette peeks inside the room. She waves at Yvette. The ghost waves back.

"You can see her, too?" you ask, holding Crikey closer.

"Don't be rude," responds Grandma Yolette, nodding. "Introduce yourself."

*Turn to page 7.*

You look back into your bedroom. A burst of bright light catches your attention. The gleaming light comes from Yvette's open hands. You look into the light and see a mountainous island hovering above her palms.

You recognize the island and the mountains. You saw them as your plane landed here. There are no mountains back home in Florida. The mountains in Yvette's hands seem to touch the clouds.

*Mòn yo rele ou,* says Yvette. *The mountains are calling you.*

"What do you mean the mountains are calling me?" you ask, putting Crikey on your shoulder.

The ghost widens her hands. The image extends with her movement. Your whole room lights up with her warm glow.

*Turn to the next page.*

You take a closer look. The island seems so real. Palm trees sway. Birds soar. Waves crash against the shore. It is not a picture. The island is alive!

"May I?" you ask, looking from Yvette to your grandma. They both nod.

You reach out and touch the glowing picture and WHOOSH! You feel wind on your face. Birds fly high in the sky. You smell salt from the ocean.

What just happened?

A moist, dense forest separates you from the great mountains that stand in the distance.

You suck in your breath as you realize: you are no longer in the bedroom at your grandma's.

*Turn to page 10.*

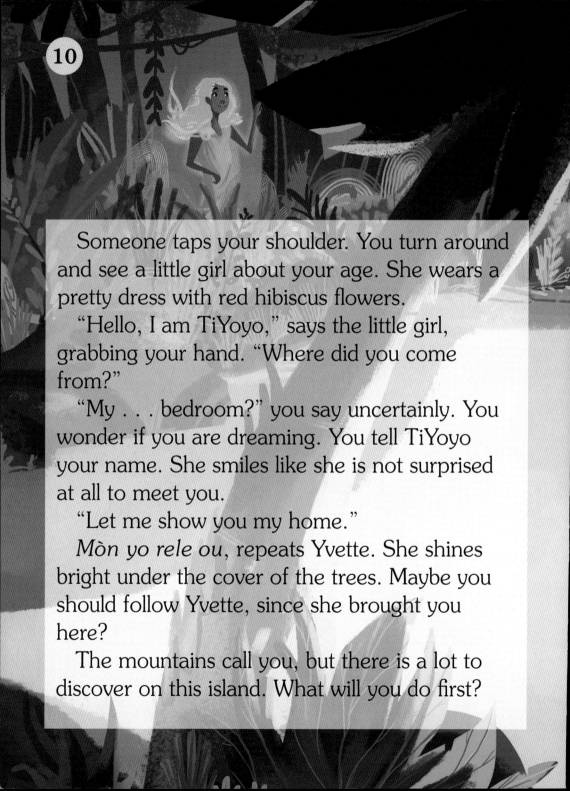

Someone taps your shoulder. You turn around and see a little girl about your age. She wears a pretty dress with red hibiscus flowers.

"Hello, I am TiYoyo," says the little girl, grabbing your hand. "Where did you come from?"

"My . . . bedroom?" you say uncertainly. You wonder if you are dreaming. You tell TiYoyo your name. She smiles like she is not surprised at all to meet you.

"Let me show you my home."

*Mòn yo rele ou*, repeats Yvette. She shines bright under the cover of the trees. Maybe you should follow Yvette, since she brought you here?

The mountains call you, but there is a lot to discover on this island. What will you do first?

*If you travel to the mountains with Yvette, turn to the next page.*

*If you take a look around the island with the little girl TiYoyo, turn to page 38.*

"Maybe another time!" you tell TiYoyo politely. You approach the ghost, Yvette. Your grandmother knew this ghost. You think you can trust her.

"Take me to the mountains!" you tell the ghost. She sets off into the forest, and you follow her.

*Go on to the next page.*

You must travel through the forest to reach the mountains. You look to the mountains while you run after Yvette. The peaks reach up toward the great blue sky. They almost touch the clouds!

*Turn to page 15.*

As you run, you feel a rhythm beneath your feet. Boom-a-boom-a-boom. Boom. Boom-a-boom-a-boom. Boom. You hold onto Crikey. His body shakes to the beat. You open your mouth to ask Yvette about the strange rhythm, but a new voice in your head surprises you.

*Welcome*, says the gentle voice.

"Who said that?" you ask. You glance around the forest. Yvette shrugs at you, and she is silent. There is no one else around.

*Turn to page 17.*

One of the trees bows toward you. It points toward its trunk. *I did*, it says.

*Turn to the next page.*

"Ahh!" you shout, surprised by the talking tree. You stumble backward and trip over a rock. Crikey flies from your hands through the air.

The startled iguana is caught by one of the tree's branches. Another branch tries to catch you, but it tears through your sleeve. You fall onto the dirt. Boom-a-boom-a-boom. Boom. Boom-a-boom-a-boom. Boom. You feel the rhythm in your hands. In your bruised knees. In the tips of your toes. The rhythm is coming from the dirt!

*Go on to the next page.*

You look from the talking trees to the magical booming dirt. Last, you stare at the friendly ghost. "What is going on?" you wonder aloud.

*If you ask about the talking trees, turn to the next page.*

*If you ask about the magical dirt, turn to page 33.*

*If you ask about the friendly ghost, turn to page 42.*

A tree branch drops in front of you. The branch pulls you to your feet.

*Have no fear*, says the tree.

"I'm not scared," you say. You are not afraid, but you are confused. "How are you talking? How are you moving?"

*Nothing is ordinary on this island*, says the tree. *Not even you.*

The tree drops Crikey into your arms. You put your iguana on your shoulder.

"I guess the magic explains how the mountains are calling me," you say. "But I still don't know *why* they are calling me."

*You will know the answer soon enough.*

Yvette appears by your side. All the trees bow toward you, offering their branches.

*Would you like us to help you reach the mountains?* they ask.

---

*If you decide to accept the trees' help, turn to the next page.*

*If you decide to keep walking through the forest, turn to page 34.*

"Yes, please help me," you say to the trees. You stay still as they lift you gently into their strong branches.

The first tree passes you to the next tree, and you move through the forest. You hold on tight to Crikey. You soar from one tree to the next.

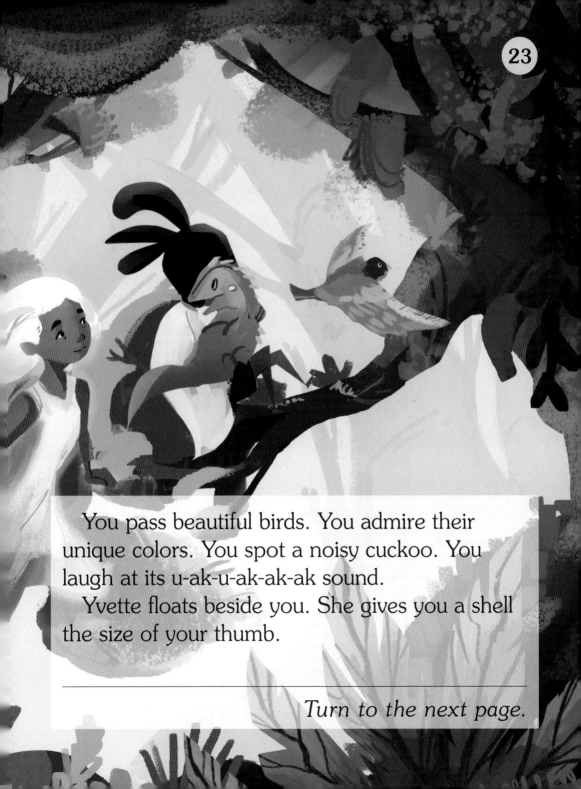

You pass beautiful birds. You admire their unique colors. You spot a noisy cuckoo. You laugh at its u-ak-u-ak-ak-ak sound.

Yvette floats beside you. She gives you a shell the size of your thumb.

*Turn to the next page.*

With its white background and colorful, spiraling stripes, the shell Yvette gives you reminds you of a candy cane. You hold it in your hand. A snail comes out of the shell. You greet your new friend with a smile.

The snail licks your fingers with its long tongue. A strange tingly feeling spreads from your fingertips to your hand. Your hand begins to change colors.

*Turn to the next page.*

You drop the snail. Stripes cover your hand in many colors. Your skin turns blue, pink, green, purple, and yellow. You wave to get Yvette's attention. The ghost floats closer to get a better look.

*Sak pase?* she asks.

"What happened?" you repeat. "*You* gave me that thing!"

*Turn to page 29.*

Before Yvette can respond, the colors swirl around and around. They form a beautiful pattern. The blue, pink, green, purple, and yellow dance on your skin.

Crikey carefully touches your hand with his tail. His tail, once green, changes with the same colors as your hand.

The trees pick up the pace. You soar faster and faster through the dense forest. The trees lower you at the foot of the mountains.

*Turn to the next page.*

*Put your hand in the dirt*, instruct the mountains. You place your colorful hand into the dirt without a second thought. Crikey does the same with his tail. Boom-a-boom-a-boom. Boom. Boom-a-boom-a-boom. Boom. A warm feeling washes over you. When you pull your hand from the magical dirt, it has returned to its normal color. Crikey's tail is green again, too.

*Go on to the next page.*

You admire your hand in the sunlight.

*At last, you have answered our call*, say the mountains. *Please make yourself at home.*

Palm trees dance in the wind. Birds soar around you. You have never felt so welcomed!

## The End

You stick your hands into the dirt. Boom-a-boom-a-boom. Boom. Boom-a-boom-a-boom. Boom.

"What is that?" you ask Yvette.

Yvette smiles a big, ghostly smile. She shines bright under the cover of the trees. She puts her hand over her chest and gestures for you to do the same.

You feel a similar rhythm beneath your shirt as the one found in the dirt. Boom-a-boom-a-boom. Boom. Boom-a-boom-a-boom. Boom.

The heart of the island beats for you.

**The End**

You decide to walk through the forest without the trees' help. To your surprise, the trees walk with you and Yvette. They follow you one by one. New trees greet and bow to you. The entire forest seems to uproot itself to join you on your journey.

"Why are they following us?" you ask Yvette.

The ghost smiles a wide, bright smile. *Sa fè lontan depi nou pa kwaze.*

You are confused. You scratch your head and glance around at the marching forest. What do they mean when they say, "long time no see"? You have never seen any of them before today.

*Go on to the next page.*

"But we never met before today," you say to Yvette. Yvette weaves in and out of the trees. Her glow flickers as she moves between the trees' shade and the gaps of sunlight.

For the first time, the ghost does not speak inside your head. Instead, she says aloud, "We have met you."

You glance down at Crikey. The iguana stares blankly at you. He does not know what Yvette means by that either.

"We have met you in your great grandmother's laugh," explains the ghost. "We have met you in your great grandfather's dance. We have met you in your Grandma Yolette's sense of adventure. We have met you in your Papa Theo's playfulness. We have met you in your mother's eyes . . . We know you because we know your beginnings. We know your roots."

*Turn to the next page.*

Roots. You know that word. Hadn't your mom mentioned getting back to your roots? Did she mean spending time with your grandma and meeting the friendly ghost? Did she mean feeling the beating dirt and walking with the talking and marching trees?

Speaking of the trees, the only roots you knew before today were the ones that kept plants in their place. But Yvette used the word differently. Were you like a tree? Was your family like roots?

*Go on to the next page.*

Thinking about the word "root," you decide that getting back to your roots means coming to Haiti for the first time and realizing the island was always a part of you. It is a part of you because it is a part of your family.

*Eske w konprann?* ask the trees.

You nod and smile because you do understand.

As you reach the mountains with the friendly ghost and marching trees, you understand why the mountains summoned you to the island.

**The End**

"I want to go with TiYoyo," you tell Yvette. The ghost nods and disappears.

"Come on," says TiYoyo, pulling you by the hand.

The two of you run through the forest. The wind kisses your cheeks as you race.

Soon, the smell of salt fills your nostrils. You breathe the scent in deep. There's an ocean nearby, but where?

You run until there are no more trees.

*Turn to page 40.*

You and TiYoyo reach the beach. There is a big, blue ocean in front of you. The sea is turquoise and royal blue. It sparkles like diamonds in the sunlight.

TiYoyo leaves you to stare at the wonderful sight. She kicks off her sandals and frolics along the shoreline. She splashes in the water, giggling with joy.

You step onto the soft white sand. The sand dances beneath your toes. The rhythm of the sand dance is fast. It's wild and free.

*Go on to the next page.*

The sand moves you left and right. You glide on it like you're riding a surfboard. Left. Right. Back and forth. The sand is asking you to join its dance, but the water looks so inviting!

*If you run to the sparkling water, turn to page 48.*

*If you dance with the sand, turn to page 55.*

"What is going on?" you ask the friendly ghost.

*Fon ti chita*, says Yvette, asking you to sit.

You sit down and cradle Crikey in your arms.

You feel the rhythm in the dirt against your skin. The trees eavesdrop, bending around you and Yvette. The ghost's glow is stronger under the thick leaves.

You settle into your seat, preparing for Yvette's explanation.

*Turn to page 50.*

You stare at the little girl in front of you with wide eyes. The dress. The laughter. She even has a similar bun on the top of her head.

"Grandma?" you ask.

"Clever child," says TiYoyo, transforming back into your Grandma Yolette. "I knew you would figure it out!"

## The End

Grandma Yolette has a delicious plate waiting for you when you return. She has even prepared a small plate of leaves for Crikey.

*Go on to the next page.*

Although it feels like only a short while has passed since you were asleep in your bedroom, you have been gone with Yvette for a full day. You missed breakfast and lunch. No wonder your stomach rumbled like thunder!

You quickly wash your hands and dig into your food. When you finish your first helping, Grandma Yolette refills your empty plate.

*Turn to the next page.*

Your grandma watches you scarf down your second helping.

"How was your trip?" she asks.

"Amazing!" you exclaim, before adding, "I wish you were there."

"I *was* there," says Grandma Yolette with a sly smile. She twirls in her pretty dress with its lovely red flowers. You remember the little girl who tapped you on the shoulder. Your mouth drops open. You knew her dress looked familiar!

**The End**

You join TiYoyo near the sparkling water. You splash and dance along the shore. The waves crash against you. Water shines like glitter on your skin.

"Isn't it wonderful?" asks TiYoyo.

"It's incredible!"

You splash water at TiYoyo and she splashes water back at you. The two of you laugh. TiYoyo slaps her knees as she chuckles. Curious. Your grandma does the same thing when she laughs.

The red flowers on TiYoyo's dress catch your attention again. They seem so familiar. Almost as familiar as the little girl herself.

*If you ask about the red flowers,
turn to page 52.*

*If you ask about TiYoyo,
turn to page 56.*

Yvette readies her hands to speak. A warm light shimmers above her palms. A loud rumble in your stomach startles the ghost. The light fades as quickly as it arrived.

"*Mwen grangou,*" you say shyly. "I'm hungry."

A bright light appears in Yvette's palms.

*Go on to the next page.*

The light slowly splits in two. There is one above each of Yvette's palms.

In the ghost's left hand, your Grandma Yolette cooks over a small fire.

In the ghost's right hand, a pathway leads into the heart of the mountains.

Your stomach growls again, rumbling like thunder in your belly. Which is more powerful: your appetite for food or your appetite for adventure?

*If you return home for dinner, turn to page 44.*

*If you travel into the heart of the mountains, turn to page 58.*

"Why do those flowers look so familiar?" you ask, pointing at the red flowers on TiYoyo's dress.

"They are all over the island," answers TiYoyo. "They represent joy in your life."

"They are very pretty," you say, before adding, "That is a very nice dress."

"*Mèsi, ma chérie*," says TiYoyo.

*Chérie?* Why would someone your age call you darling? Only your aunties, older cousins, or grandma have called you *chérie*.

*Turn to page 43.*

"Would you like to help me collect seashells?" you ask.

"Sure," says TiYoyo. "What will you do with the shells after we collect them?"

"I'm going to make a necklace for my grandma," you say, plucking beautiful shells out of the soft white sand. "I want to thank her for letting me visit."

"I'm sure she will like that," says TiYoyo, giving you a handful of colorful seashells.

"I hope she does," you say, putting the shells in your pocket. "Then maybe I can come back next summer!"

**The End**

You dance with the sand.
Step left. Step back. Glide to the right.
Step left. Step forward. Glide to the right.
Step back. Glide to the left. Step right.
Step forward. Glide to the left.

The sand keeps up with you as you dance. It moves as you move. Its energy reaches you. You feel joyous. Light. Free.

TiYoyo leaves the water and joins in on the fun. She struggles with your made-up dance moves, but you and the sand help her as best as you can. Her feet get lost in the movements. She falls. You help her up.

As the two of you dance with the sand, you cannot contain your laughter. TiYoyo dances just like your grandma!

**The End**

"Have we met before?" you ask TiYoyo. The little girl glances from the water and grins at you.

"I don't know," she teases. "Have we?"

"You seem very familiar," you say. "But I cannot figure out why."

*Go on to the next page.*

"Do I remind you of anyone?" she questions, smiling softly.

You scratch your head. Would your new friend understand if you told her that she reminds you of your grandma?

*If you change the subject,
turn to page 53.*

*If you answer TiYoyo's question honestly,
turn to page 64.*

You shush your rumbling stomach and reach for the ghost's left hand.

WHOOSH! You travel into the heart of the mountains. Yvette takes you there very fast!

The heart of the mountains is a dark cave with beautiful red hibiscus flowers that shine beneath Yvette's warm glow.

"I didn't know flowers grew inside mountains," you say, touching the flowers' soft petals.

Yvette shakes her head from side to side. *The flowers are a gift.*

*Turn to the next page.*

"*Mèsi*," you say, thanking the kind ghost. You smell a flower before placing it behind your ear.

You walk around the heart of the mountains. Yvette watches you explore. She hovers patiently in the middle of the cave. She shines brighter and brighter as she watches you.

*Go on to the next page.*

You run your hand along the ridged walls. A deep rumbling knocks you off your feet. *Wow!* You didn't think you were *that* hungry.

You lean on the wall as you pick yourself up.

The rumbling increases. Strange. It is not coming from your stomach, but from the mountains. Stranger, the rumbling feels like laughter.

*Turn to the next page.*

*Enough*, laugh the mountains.

You cannot believe it. The mountains are ticklish!

You glance at Yvette. The ghost covers her hand with her mouth as she chuckles.

You grin a wide, mischievous grin. You secure Crikey in one arm. You plant your feet. Then, you run your free hand along the walls. You race from one side of the cave to the other.

*Go on to the next page.*

*Ha, ha, ha*, giggle the mountains.

Soon, the heart of the mountains rumbles with your laughter too.

## The End

"You remind me of my grandma," you say to the little girl. TiYoyo crosses her arms against her chest.

"See, you're standing like her!" you exclaim, pointing. "And you called me *chérie* like her!"

TiYoyo covers her mouth.

"And you're covering your mouth because you even laugh like her," you say, pulling TiYoyo's hand away. TiYoyo lets out a laugh. She slaps her knee and wipes tears from her eyes with the back of her hand. She transforms back into your Grandma Yolette.

"I knew it was you, Grandma!" you say, giving her a great big hug.

**The End**

## ABOUT THE ARTIST

**Manuel Mal** is a Filipino artist who makes children's book-styled illustrations and illustrates mainly on digital media, using Sai and Procreate. When he was a child, he looked at the storybooks his parents bought for him and remembers being amazed at all the pretty pictures. He used to spend a lot of time just admiring the art and seeing how cool all the little details were. So now he decided to try and do the same thing.

## ABOUT THE AUTHOR

**Kyandreia Jones** is a Posse Miami Scholar and graduate of Hamilton College, where she received her BA in creative writing. She was born and raised in south Florida. When she thinks of home she likes to muse that she is in a "sunshine state of mind." Her latest CYOA® book, *The Ghost on the Mountain*, discusses home, belonging, and the magic of knowing your roots. Jones has always been proud of her ancestors. She often summons the strength of her maternal grandparents, who planted the seeds of their hope and faith in their children and grandchildren. She finds inspiration and courage in their tales of leaving Haiti to cultivate a better future for their children, one with the potential to flourish and grow in foreign soil. So too, she calls forth the resilience of her paternal grandparents, who forged a similarly bright future for their loved ones. Writing a book that both sides of her family can appreciate and enjoy has been the most beautiful endeavor of Jones's career. Alongside her trusty pup pal Noble, Jones continues her career as a freelance writer, educator, and public speaker. She is currently also pursuing a career in TV/film as a screenwriter. Jones values reading, writing, laughing, and promoting universal kindness.

**For games, activities, and other fun stuff, or to write to Kyandreia, visit us online at CYOA.com**

# CHECK OFF THE BOOKS THAT YOU HAVE READ FROM THE
## CHOOSE YOUR OWN ADVENTURE® DRAGONLARK SERIES

☆ Princess Island

☆ Princess Perri and the Second Summer

☆ Unicorn Princess

☆ Your Very Own Robot

☆ Your Very Own Robot Goes Cuckoo-Bananas!

☆ Gus Vs. The Robot King

☆ Dino Lab

☆ Dragon Day

☆ Search for the Dragon Queen

☆ The Lake Monster Mystery

☆ Monsters of the Deep

☆ Ghost Island

☆ Sand Castle

☆ Your Grandparents Are Spies

☆ Your Grandparents Are Zombies!

☆ Your Grandparents Are Ninjas

☆ Your Grandparents Are Werewolves

☆ Fire!

☆ Lost Dog!

☆ Space Pup

☆ The Haunted House

☆ Return To Haunted House

☆ Indian Trail

☆ Owl Tree

☆ Your Purrr-fect Birthday

☆ Caravan

☆ Mermaid Island

☆ Your Baby Unicorn

☆ Fairy House

☆ The Ghost on the Mountain

# GUS

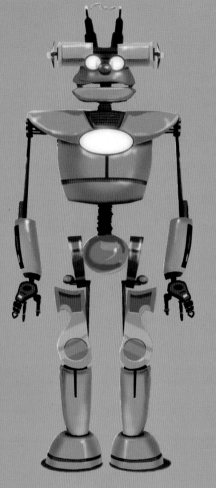

**Age:** 2

**Favorite food:**
ice cream

**Likes:** ice cream,
causing trouble

**Dislikes:**
junkyards,
water

## You can find me in:
Your Very Own Robot
Your Very Own Robot Goes Cuckoo-Bananas
Gus Vs. The Robot King

# HOMER

**YOU CAN FIND ME IN:**
SPACE PUP
LOST DOG!
HAUNTED HOUSE
RETURN TO HAUNTED HOUSE

**AGE:** in human or dog years?
**FAVORITE FOOD:** pizza
**LIKES:** time travel, french poodles, chewing shoes
**DISLIKES:** vacuums and the mail carrier

# Princess Peregrine Yvette

## AKA Princess Perri

**You can find me in:**

Princess Island

Princess Perri and the Second Summer

Unicorn Princess

**Age:** 9

**Favorite color:** yellow

**Likes:** cooking, fixing stuff, the outdoors

**Dislikes:** fancy ball gowns and being a princess

# Sirena

**Favorite food:** Seaweed salad

**Hobbies:** Protecting our oceans, swimming with turtles, playing pranks on land princes

YOU CAN FIND ME IN... MERMAID ISLAND

# SUNNY

**FAVORITE FOOD:** BLUEBERRIES

**BEST FRIEND:** YOU

**FAVORITE COLOR:** RAINBOW

YOU CAN FIND ME IN... YOUR BABY UNICORN